I t had been rumored that twelve ancient gold goblets were hidden in the city of Huddlesford. Over the years, many came to seek them, but without success.

In *The Great Treasure Hunt*, Pembleton Derby, the mysterious man in blue, found and claimed the golden goblets as his own, moments before the treasure hunter, Sir Gordon Goodfellow, reached the goal. When Pembleton—the richest man in the world—vanished in a hot-air balloon, it was revealed that he was making a gift of the goblets to the International Museum. But where are the fabled goblets? The treasure hunter decides to search all of Pembleton Derby's twelve homes throughout the world to find the goblets.

Join Sir Gordon Goodfellow on his quest and you, too, may become a great treasure hunter. As you travel around the world you will find all of the items listed under each picture, and finally, if you are successful, the twelve golden goblets.

SIMON & SCHUSTER BOOKS FOR YOUNG READERS
An imprint of Simon & Schuster Children's Publishing Division
1230 Avenue of the Americas
New York, New York 10020
Copyright © 1995 by David Anson Russo
All rights reserved including the right of reproduction in whole or in part in any form.
SIMON & SCHUSTER BOOKS FOR YOUNG READERS
is a trademark of Simon & Schuster.
The text for this book is set in 18-point Usherwood.
The illustrations were done in watercolor.
Manufactured in the United States of America

10 9 8 7 6 5 4 3 2 1

ISBN: 0-689-80281-1

DAVID ANSON RUSSO

AROUND THE WORLD:
The Great Treasure Hunt

SIMON & SCHUSTER BOOKS FOR YOUNG READERS

In Hawaii, find the treasure hunter.

In Russia, find the treasure hunter and **2** clocks.

In Egypt, find the treasure hunter, **2** clocks, and **3** arrows.

In Italy, find the treasure hunter, **2** clocks, **3** arrows, and **4** bandits.

In England, find the treasure hunter, **2** clocks, **3** arrows, **4** bandits, and **5** white dogs.

In Alaska, find the treasure hunter, **2** clocks, **3** arrows, **4** bandits, **5** white dogs, and **6** scissors.

In Japan, find the treasure hunter, **2** clocks, **3** arrows, **4** bandits, **5** white dogs, **6** scissors, and **7** yellow hats.

In Brazil, find the treasure hunter, **2** clocks, **3** arrows, **4** bandits,
5 white dogs, **6** scissors, **7** yellow hats, and **8** candelabra.

In France, find the treasure hunter, **2** clocks, **3** arrows, **4** bandits,
5 white dogs, **6** scissors, **7** yellow hats, **8** candelabra, and **9** green books.

In Holland, find the treasure hunter, **2** clocks, **3** arrows, **4** bandits, **5** white dogs, **6** scissors, **7** yellow hats, **8** candelabra, **9** green books, and **10** apples.

DERBYS' GOOD'AY SURPLUS OUTPOST

BUY & SELL

In Australia, find the treasure hunter, **2** clocks, **3** arrows, **4** bandits, **5** white dogs, **6** scissors, **7** yellow hats, **8** candelabra, **9** green books, **10** apples, and **11** brooms.

In China, find the treasure hunter, **2** clocks, **3** arrows, **4** bandits, **5** white dogs, **6** scissors, **7** yellow hats, **8** candelabra, **9** green books, **10** apples, **11** brooms, and **12** goblets.

Note: Meet Dexter Derby, Pembleton's father. Since Pembleton has been missing, Dexter has been on the trail of the valuable thirteenth goblet. Once the goblet is found, the final mystery will be solved. Find the white letter in each picture. Put them together to spell out the clue to finding the thirteenth goblet.